'Twas the night before Christmas
in New England's states.
In the state of Vermont,
a boy patiently waits,

Gazing out of his window
this calm, snowy night.
Would Santa Claus find him
and help with his plight?

THE
NIGHT BEFORE
CHRISTMAS
IN NEW ENGLAND

Sue Carabine

Illustrations by
Shauna Mooney Kawasaki

Gibbs Smith, Publisher
Salt Lake City

First Edition
08 07 06 05 04   5 4 3 2 1

Published by
Gibbs Smith, Publisher
P.O. Box 667
Layton, Utah 84041

1.800.748.5439 orders
www.gibbs-smith.com

Designed and produced by
  Mary Ellen Thompson, TTA Designs
Printed and bound in China

ISBN 1-58685-449-6

A few moments later
up on his rooftop,
A sleigh with eight reindeer
gently came to a stop.

Over white-steepled churches
St. Nicholas had flown,
To visit small Jerry
and make himself known!

Santa slid down the chimney,
to young Jerry's glee,
Then answered Jerry's questions
as he sat on Nick's knee.

"So you want to be great,
to be one of a kind?
Well, hop on my sleigh, lad,
let's see what we find."

Jerry hung on real tight.
They zoomed fast as a plane
And were soon gazing down on
the Pine Tree State—Maine!

The cities all sparkled—
Portland, Brunswick, and Bath—
As Christmas lights shimmered
down each little path.

"Each Christmas, a young boy
from here always asked,"
Santa chuckled, "for hiking gear,
a compass, and maps!

"Now, Robby had dreams to be
strong, brave, and bold.
Guess what? He showed up
at the frosty North Pole!

"'I'm the first one to find you,'
I remember he said,
Using dogs 'stead of reindeer
for pulling his sled!

If you study your history,
  his name is right there:
  Robert Peary—explorer,
  one most extraordinaire!"

Santa pointed out Portland
and Longfellow's home,
"Down there, little Henry
thought up his first poem!

"He was just about your age,
with one great desire:
That many would read them
and be greatly inspired!"

And so, on their travels
they left Maine far behind,
This eve the most thrilling
of young Jerry's lifetime!

Then things got exciting
as New Hampshire drew near.
Jerry saw Santa grin
'neath his fluffy white beard.

"That's where I spend summer,"
cried Santa, with glee,
"At a village near Conway—
Mrs. Santa and me!

"We love to come here to
the great Granite State.
Especially at Christmas
we simply can't wait

To place elf-made toys
around trees in the den,
From Concord to Ashland
to old Bethlehem."

At Franconia Notch,
Santa's sleigh gently hovered
O'er high Cannon Mount in
White Mountains, snow-covered.

New England's fall beauty
is one of a kind,
In winter at Christmas
most people will find

An exquisite picture
of carpets of snow,
And colored lights twinkling
with holiday glow.

Nick cried, "Massachusetts!
We'll be real busy here.
The girls and the boys are
just brimming with cheer

"In Lawrence and Greenfield
and quaint old Cape Cod.
You should know about Sammy,"
chuckled Nick, with a nod.

"It was quite a while back
on a cold winter's night,
Mrs. Claus was complaining
that all was not right.

"The thing she loves most
(of course, not counting me)
Is to sit down and rest
with a nice cup of tea!

"Well, imagine her shock
when she went to the store
And found tea would cost
nearly 50 cents more!

"'We can't afford that,'
she confided to me,
'What am I to do now
without my milk tea?'"

"Well, I told my friend Sammy,
who took it to task.
When asked what was planned,
he said quickly, 'Don't ask!'

"Now, how did I know that
he'd round up some guys
To dress up like Mohawks?
What a crazy disguise!

"And so Samuel Adams
and his Boston 'tea party'
Are remembered forever
as a group hale and hearty!"

Then Jerry and Nick left
the Bay State quite late
To traverse Connecticut,
the Constitution State.

O'er Hartford they soared—
what a beautiful sight,
Like Christmas in England
on this sacred Yule night.

Then Santa remembered
Jerry's favorite book,
Whose author had lived here.
"Let's take a quick look!

"My elves wrote some stories,"
teased Nick, looking merry.
"Have you heard of Tom Sawyer
and young Huckleberry?"

Nick's eyes were a-twinkling
when he finally laughed.
"You mean Mark Twain lived
just down there?" Jerry gasped.

Nick nodded, then queried,
"And wouldn't you know?
It's also the home of
Ms. Harriet Beecher Stowe!"

Next Danbury and Bridgeport
and New Haven's Yale,
With ivy-clad buildings
where learning prevails!

Together they sailed through
clouds wispy with snow.
On leaving they glimpsed
Mystic's tall ships below!

After a moment,
Nick touched Jerry's sleeve.
"That's Newport, Rhode Island,
down there, I believe!"

He tugged on the reins,
"What a glorious sight—
The shimmering water
reflecting Yule lights.

"My elves love to visit
this snug Ocean State,
and tour RISD,
a design school first rate,

"Whose Providence students
design loads of toys.
My elves take and build them
for all girls and boys!

"We love 'Little Rhody,'
this smallest of states,
With a heart big as Christmas.
Each year we can't wait!

"Your Green Mountain State
of Vermont is next, lad,
Where a very dear friend
of mine had a cool pad:

"An artist renowned for
his wonderful works,
Norm painted my portrait
(just one of the perks)."

"So follow your dreams, boy,"
Nick said, gliding home.
"Hear the ringing?" asked Jerry.
"I must answer that phone."

Excited, he told Nick,
"It's Ben, my best friend!
He wants me to help him
to start a new trend.

"'Together,' Ben says,
'we can share in a dream.'
We'll sell his great-grandma's
best homemade ice cream!"

Well, Santa was chuckling
as he flew out of sight.
"Merry Christmas, New England;
everybody sleep tight!"